1549

A Dog Called Dad

Story by Frank B. Edwards
Illustrated by John Bianchi

Bungalo Books

Bungalo
Books

To Small the Cat, who followed
the call of the coyotes

Illustrated by John Bianchi
Written by Frank B. Edwards
© 1994 by Bungalo Books

Canadian Cataloguing in Publication Data

Edwards, Frank B., 1952–
  A dog called dad

ISBN 0-921285-35-3 (bound)   ISBN 0-921285-34-5 (pbk.)

I. Bianchi, John   II. Title.

PS8559.D84D64 1994   jC813'.54   C94-900430-8
PZ10.3.E49Do 1994

Published in Canada by:
Bungalo Books
Box 129
Newburgh, Ontario
KOK 2S0

Co-published in U.S.A. by:
Firefly Books (U.S.) Inc.
Ellicott Station
P.O. Box 1338
Buffalo, New York
14205

Trade Distribution by:
Firefly Books Ltd.
250 Sparks Avenue
Willowdale, Ontario
M2H 2S4

Printed in Canada by:
Friesen Printers
Altona, Manitoba

coy·ote [ki-ot] *Canis latrans (barking dog)*, a small wolf renowned for its cunning and night-time hunting skills; a chicken-thieving varmint

I was only a baby when the coyotes stole my Dad.

Mom was upset at the time, of course, but I was really too young to notice.

We live on a chicken farm at the edge of the desert. The desert isn't really a good place to raise chickens, but the coyotes always seemed to like it. Every so often, they would sneak down from the hills to grab some chickens.

One night, they took Dad instead.

"There's not much we can do, I suppose," Mom said. "I just hope they take good care of him."

Over the years, Mom almost gave up hope of ever seeing Dad again, but every now and then, we would spot his silhouette against a full moon, surrounded by his fellow coyotes, howling mournfully.

"That's my Dad," I would say.

Visitors would feel tears of pity well up in their eyes. They would ruffle my hair and say, "You poor sweet thing. So brave…"

But one night when I was about 8, Dad came back. He didn't mean to. It just sort of happened. Some coyotes had come down from the hills to steal a few chickens, and as they crawled under the wire fence, Dad's tail got caught, and he couldn't get loose. It wasn't really a tail at all, just a long, tangly ponytail, but when you're a Dad being raised by coyotes, you do whatever you can to fit in with the pack.

There was a lot of yipping and yapping when he got stuck, so Mom and I went outside, and there was Dad looking pretty sheepish, wagging his ponytail at us.

"Tom, you've come back after all these years," cried Mom as she rushed toward him.

"Woof," said Dad.

Although he seemed glad to see us, we put him on a leash and kept him in the barn that night, just to be on the safe side.

Unfortunately, while it was a pretty good idea, it wasn't a great one. The next morning, Dad was still there but three chickens were missing!

It took a long time, but eventually, we housebroke him,
and he started sleeping at the foot of Mom's bed each night.

Every breakfast, Dad would join us at the table for eggs…

…then he would follow me to the school-bus stop.

Often, he would ride into town with Mom when she went shopping. He loved riding in that truck.

Dad didn't start talking until years later, but we guessed that the coyotes had originally stolen him to replace one of the adult males in the pack. He had never been a very good hunter, so he ended up playing with the pups most of the time. As a coyote, he didn't amount to much, I guess, but they liked having him around and took pretty good care of him.

He was more fun than most of my friends' fathers. He liked to play all day, and he hated baths as much as I did. Of course, I wasn't always rolling in garbage. Mom was often too busy cleaning him to even notice me at bath time.

As I got older, though, and spent less time playing with Dad, he seemed to lose interest in the farm. He started chasing cars and would sometimes disappear into the wash behind the house for hours. Once, he stayed away a whole day.

"You are going to have to spend more time with your father," Mom told me one night. "He's getting bored and has no one to play with."

I tried to teach him some grown-up tricks, but he wasn't interested. He wouldn't beg or bark thank-you, and he would roll over only if he had an itchy back. One day, I tried to play catch with him, but he wouldn't bring back the ball. He just headed over a hill out of sight with it. When I finally found him, he was racing around with a bunch of coyotes. They were playing tag and didn't see me.

I realized then that Dad missed his buddies.

That night, Mom and I ate our dinner on the porch and put out some extra plates of stewed chicken. Within minutes, Dad and half a dozen slobbering coyotes came racing out of the shadows.

After dessert, I got out Mom's banjo and my harmonica, and we played until the moon rose above the cabin. Then Dad and the others took over, howling and singing like never before. It lasted until the moon sank out of sight.

"We'll have to do that more often," I said as I did the dishes. Dad's ears perked up, and I knew that we were about to start a long tradition. And sure enough, every night of the full moon since then, we have had a good old-fashioned hoot and howl.

Over the years, people have come from all over to watch us carry on with those wild coyotes, and Mom has turned it into quite a show. She gave up raising chickens for good, and there's even talk of a Hollywood movie.

But, of course, Dad hasn't changed much. He's still the same old dog he's always been.